From the acclaimed duo **Dianna Hutts Aston** and **Sylvia Long**
comes this gorgeous and informative introduction to the world of butterflies.
From the tiny Arian Small Blue to the grand Queen Alexandra's Birdwing,
an incredible variety of butterflies are celebrated here in all
their beauty and wonder.

Poetic in voice and elegant in design, this book introduces children
to an astounding array of butterfly facts, making it equally at home in a
classroom reading circle as it is being read to a child on a parent's lap.

PRAISE FOR *A BUTTERFLY IS PATIENT*

"Beautiful . . . invites 5- to 10-year-olds to enjoy the variety,
complexity, and sumptuousness of natural things." —*The Wall Street Journal*

"Vivid and detailed." —*The Washington Post*

★ "A lyrical, colorful, and elegant production."
—*School Library Journal*, starred review

★ "Delicate, elegant, and informative . . . Enchanting . . . A lovely mix
of science and wonder." —*Publishers Weekly*, starred review

★ "Aston and Long have again struck gold. . . . stunning in its execution."
—*Library Media Connection*, starred review

"Similar butterfly albums abound, but none show these most decorative
members of the insect clan to better advantage." —*Kirkus Reviews*

"Beautiful . . . This lovely book, well-researched and beautifully produced,
will delight butterfly-lovers both young and older." —Children's Literature

An ALA Notable Children's Book Final Reading List selection
A Bank Street College of Education Best Book of the Year Reading List selection
An IRA Teachers' Choices Reading List selection
An ALSC Notable Children's Book Nominee

Rice Paper

Anna's Eighty-Eight

Owl

Common Bluebottle

Common Birdwing

Tailed Jay

Monarch

Pipevine Swallowtail

Ruddy Daggerwing

Hieroglyphic Flat

Moonlight Jewel

Lime

Painted Jezebel

Mourning Cloak

Zebra Swallowtail

Queen Alexandra's Birdwing

Great Purple Hairstreak

Common Posy

Blue Mormon

Peacock

Orange Oakleaf

Eastern Tiger Swallowtail

Malay Lacewing

Green Baron

Elbowed Pierrot

Blue Morpho

Spotted Fritillary

Diana Fritillary

American Copper

Zebra Longwing

Common Mormon

Common Buckeye

For my Sri Lankan friend and diviner of codes,
Dilshan Madawala. —D. H. A.

For my father—Frank J. Carlisle, Jr.—the blue-eyed
sailor, who is my source for all things wise and wonderful.
Among other things, he taught me the value of an interest
in the natural world and our place in it. —S. L.

Blue-Eyed Sailor

ACKNOWLEDGMENTS:

Victoria Rock, editor, and Sara Gillingham, book designer,
for their wisdom and dedication to quality in children's books.

Jeffrey S. Pippen, Nicholas School of the Environment, Duke University; Nicky Davis, Wild Utah Project, Butterflies
and Moths; Linden Gledhill, photographer, Philadelphia, PA; Adrian Hoskins, LearnAboutButterflies.com, Hampshire,
England; Teh Su Phin, Panang Butterfly Farm, Malaysia; Lizanne Whiteley, Conservation of Butterflies in South Africa;
Robert N. Wiedenmann, Dept. of Entomology, University of Arkansas; Silvia Mecenero, South African Butterfly
Conservation Assessment; Steve Woodhall, President, Lepidopterists' Society of Africa; Jean-Claude Petit,
Butterflies of Sangau National Park, Ecuador; Niklas Walberg, Dept. of Biology, University of Turku, Finland;
Andrg Victor Lucci Freitas, Universidade Estadual de Campinas, São Paulo, Brazil; Museum Victoria's Discover
Centre, Victoria, Australia; Gareth S. Welsh, Butterfly World, Stockton-on-Tees, England; Thomas Neubauer,
ButterflyCorner.net, Germany; John J. Obrycki, Chair, Dept. of Entomology, University of Kentucky; Halmar Taschner,
South African Nursery Assoc.; Melani Hugo, Butterfly Garden at Ludwig's Rose Farm, Gauteng, South Africa;
Tim Loh, British Columbia, Canada

First Chronicle Books LLC paperback edition, published in 2015.
Originally published in hardcover in 2011 by Chronicle Books LLC.

ISBN 978-1-4521-4124-4

The Library of Congress has cataloged the original edition as follows:
Aston, Dianna Hutts.
A butterfly is patient / by Dianna Aston ; illustrated by Sylvia Long.
p. cm.
ISBN 978-0-8118-6479-4
1. Butterflies—Juvenile literature. I. Long, Sylvia. II. Title.
QL544.2.A87 2011
595.78'9—dc22
2010008548

Manufactured in China.

MIX
Paper from
responsible sources
FSC® C104723
FSC
www.fsc.org

Book design by Sara Gillingham.
Hand lettered by Anne Robin and Sylvia Long.
The illustrations in this book were rendered in watercolor.

10 9 8 7 6 5 4

Chronicle Books LLC
680 Second Street
San Francisco, California 94107

Chronicle Books—we see things differently.
Become part of our community at www.chroniclekids.com.

Southern Dogface

Spotted Fritillary

A Butterfly Is Patient

Dianna Hutts Aston   Sylvia Long

chronicle books · san francisco

A butterfly is patient.

Great Purple Hairstreak

It begins as an egg beneath an umbrella of leaves,
protected from rain, hidden from creatures that might
harm it . . . until the caterpillar inside chews free
from its egg case, tiny, wingless, hungry to grow.

A butterfly is creative.

A caterpillar feeds on leaves, eating so much that it must *molt*, or shed its skin, many times. It can grow up to 30,000 times larger than it was when it took its first bite.

1ST INSTAR

15 DAYS

3RD INSTAR

21 DAYS

5TH INSTAR

26 DAYS

PREPUPA

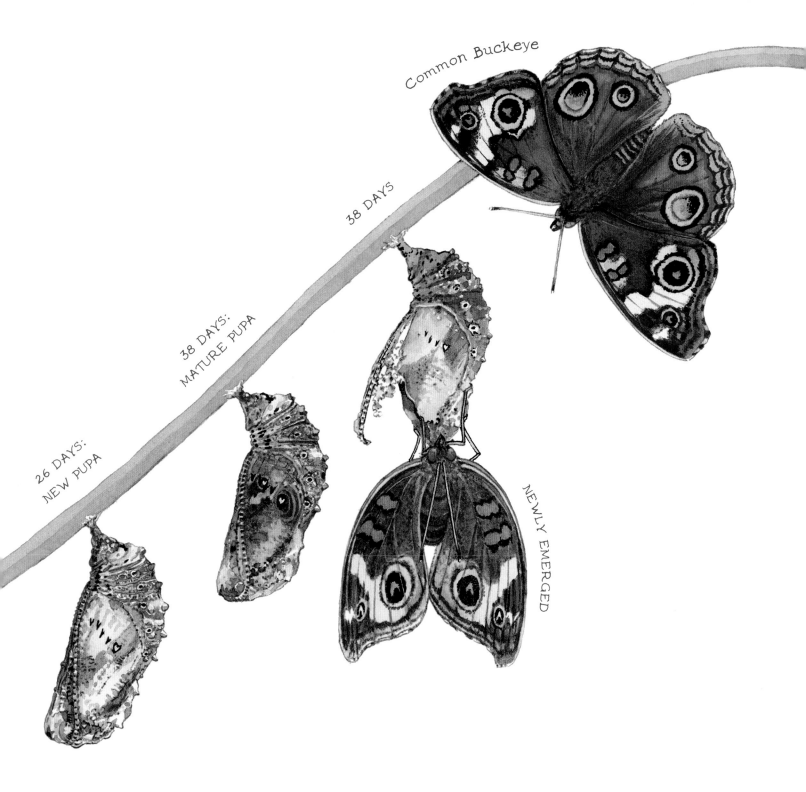

Common Buckeye

38 DAYS

38 DAYS: MATURE PUPA

26 DAYS: NEW PUPA

NEWLY EMERGED

Once a caterpillar has eaten all that it needs, it creates a protective covering called a *chrysalis*. Curled inside the chrysalis, it is growing wings. Now it is time for *metamorphosis*, changing from one form to another.

Zebra Longwing

Eastern Tiger Swallowtail

A butterfly is helpful.

Butterflies, like bees, help pollinate plants so that they can reproduce, or make seeds. As a butterfly flits from flower to flower, sipping nectar, tiny grains of pollen cling to its body, then fall away onto other flowers. Seeds are only produced when pollen is transferred between flowers of the same species. This is called *pollination*.

Owl

A butterfly is protective.

Peacock

Butterflies use their wings to protect themselves from predators such as hungry birds, lizards, and other insects. Some butterflies have markings on their wings called *eyespots*. Scientists don't know what they are used for—perhaps to scare away predators or attract mates!

Orange Oakleaf

Wings can help butterflies *camouflage*,
or hide, themselves in the environment.
One kind of butterfly, the peacock butterfly,
makes a hissing sound by rubbing its
wings together when it is alarmed.

Pipevine Swallowtail

A butterfly is poisonous.

Monarch

The warning colors of some butterflies' wings—yellows,
reds, oranges, whites, and blacks—tell predators that
they are poisonous or bad-tasting. Monarchs and Pipevine
Swallowtails eat poisonous plants as caterpillars so
that they become poisonous as adults. Birds and other
insects have learned not to eat them!

Moonlight Jewel

Painted Jezebel

Green Baron

Tailed Jay

Rice Paper

Common Birdwing

Ruddy Daggerwing

A butterfly is

Anna's Eighty-Eight

Elbowed Pierrot

Blue Morpho

Common Posy

spectacular!

Hieroglyphic Flat

Zebra Swallowtail

Spotted Fritillary

Malay Lacewing

Malay Lacewing

A butterfly is thirsty.

To find flowers, butterflies smell the air with their
antennae. They taste with their feet but sip nectar,
the sweet liquid produced by many flowers, with
a *proboscis*, a "tongue" that coils and uncoils.

Lime

Some butterflies get their nourishment from rotting fruit (Blue Morpho) or minerals. Often, a kaleidoscope of butterflies gathers as a "puddle club" in mud near a pond or a lake to drink water rich in salts and minerals.

A butterfly is big . . .

The rare Queen Alexandra's Birdwing is the largest butterfly in the world, with wings that can span up to 1 foot (30.4 cm). It lives in the rain forest in northern Papua New Guinea.

Queen Alexandra's Birdwing

Arian Small Blue

or tiny.

The smallest is the rarely-seen Arian Small Blue found
in Afghanistan with a wingspan of less than one third of
an inch (8 mm), about the length of a grain of rice.

A butterfly is scaly.

A rainbow of shiny, powdery scales covers the
wings of a butterfly, scales stacked like shingles on
a roof. Without scales, its wings would be as
transparent as the wings of a bee or a dragonfly.

Satyr

The colors, patterns, and shapes of a
butterfly's wings have a purpose. Some
use their pattern of colors to attract
mates. In places where the climate is cool,
dark scales absorb heat from the sun, warming
the butterfly's flight muscles. Butterflies are
cold-blooded and must have a body temperature
of 86 degrees F (30 degrees C) to fly.

Diana Fritillary

Mourning Cloak

Zebra Longwing

A butterfly

American Copper

Butterflies and moths belong to the same family of insects, the *Lepidoptera*, which means "scale wing." They are the only insects with scaly wings, but there are differences between them.

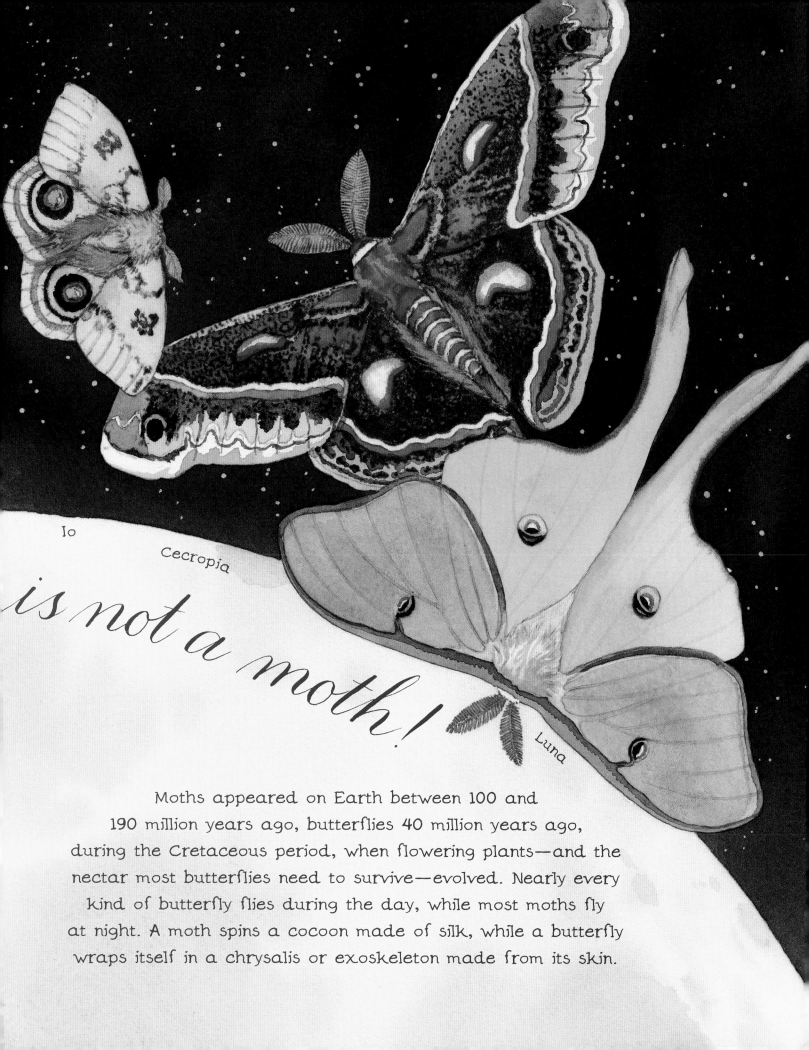

Io

Cecropia

is not a moth!

Luna

Moths appeared on Earth between 100 and
190 million years ago, butterflies 40 million years ago,
during the Cretaceous period, when flowering plants—and the
nectar most butterflies need to survive—evolved. Nearly every
kind of butterfly flies during the day, while most moths fly
at night. A moth spins a cocoon made of silk, while a butterfly
wraps itself in a chrysalis or exoskeleton made from its skin.

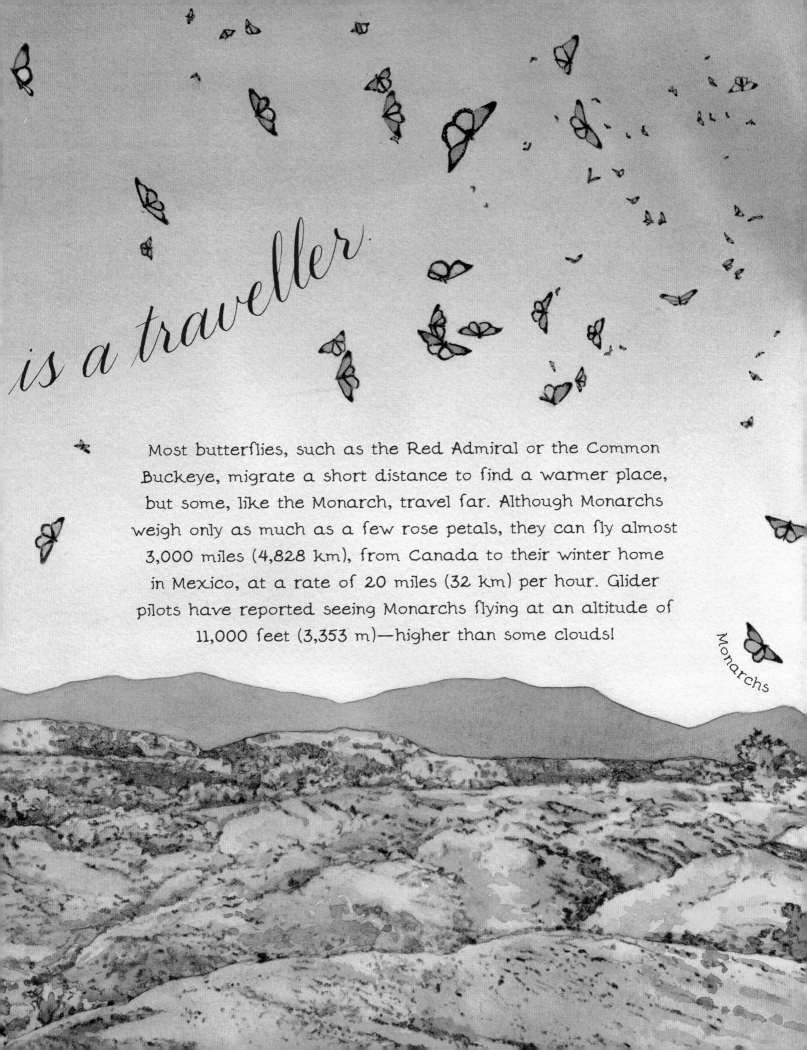

is a traveller.

Most butterflies, such as the Red Admiral or the Common Buckeye, migrate a short distance to find a warmer place, but some, like the Monarch, travel far. Although Monarchs weigh only as much as a few rose petals, they can fly almost 3,000 miles (4,828 km), from Canada to their winter home in Mexico, at a rate of 20 miles (32 km) per hour. Glider pilots have reported seeing Monarchs flying at an altitude of 11,000 feet (3,353 m)—higher than some clouds!

Monarchs

A butterfly is magical.

Monarchs gather in huge numbers in the
forests of Central Mexico waiting for spring.
Then they fly north, to the milkweed plants
in North America, where they lay their eggs.
Now it is time again for their metamorphosis.

Monarch

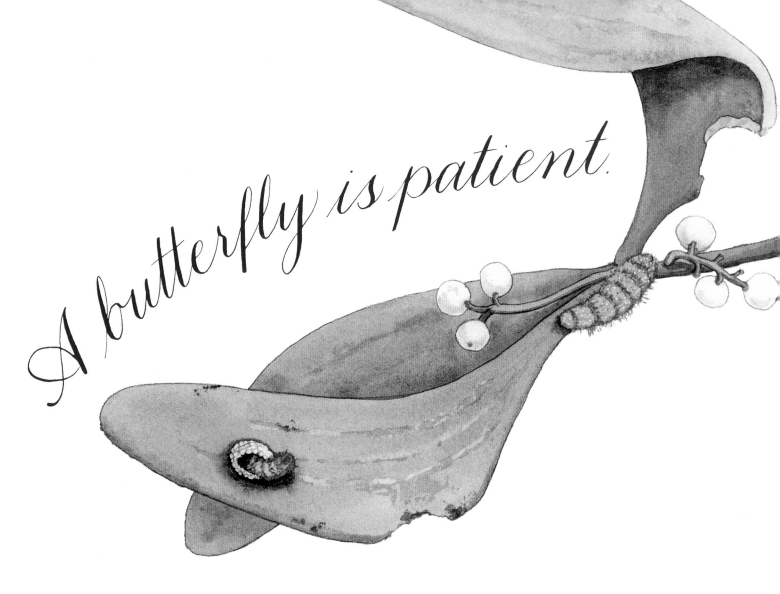

A butterfly is patient.

The egg hatches,
the caterpillar emerges,
feasting on leaves
before it wraps itself
into its warm,
protective chrysalis,

patiently waiting . . .

Great Purple Hairstreak

Great Purple Hairstreak

to soar!

American Copper

Arian Small Blue

Great Purple Hairstreak

Green Baron

Blue Morpho

Common Posy

Queen Alexandra's Birdwing

Blue Mormon

Rice Paper

Common Bluebottle

Common Buckeye

Eastern Tiger Swallowtail

Common Mormon

Elbowed Pierrot

Spotted Fritillary

Ruddy Daggerwing

Malay Lacewing

ALSO BY DIANNA HUTTS ASTON AND SYLVIA LONG:

An Egg Is Quiet

★ "A delight for budding naturalists of all stripes, flecks, dots and textures."
—*Kirkus Reviews*, starred review

★ "This attractive volume pleases on both an aesthetic and intellectual level."
—*Publishers Weekly*, starred review

"Exceptionally handsome . . . A beautiful guide to the unexpected panoply of the egg."
—*School Library Journal*

"Beautifully illustrated . . . Will inspire kids to marvel at animals' variety and beauty." —*Booklist*

A Junior Library Guild Premiere selection
A New York Public Library Title for Reading and Sharing
A Chicago Public Library Best of the Best

A Seed Is Sleepy

★ "Will stretch children's minds and imaginations." —*School Library Journal*, starred review

"Will encourage kids to wonder about the plant world's mysterious,
gorgeous spectrum of possibilities." —*Booklist*

A Rock Is Lively

★ "Eye-catching and eye-opening." —*School Library Journal*, starred review

A Boston Globe Best Children's Book of the Year
An IRA Teachers' Choices Reading List selection

For more information and classroom activities, visit www.chroniclekids.com!

DIANNA HUTTS ASTON is the author of many bestselling books for children. She is also the founder of The Oz Project, a nonprofit foundation which provides inspirational hot air balloon experiences to disadvantaged children. She lives on an island off the coast of Texas. Visit her at www.diannahaston.com.

SYLVIA LONG is the award-winning illustrator of many bestselling books for children. Her detailed paintings are inspired by her love of animals and the outdoors. She lives in Scottsdale, Arizona, with her husband and their dogs, Jackson and Truman. Visit her at www.sylvia-long.com.